I0537748

BÊTE NOIRE

FEAR IS JUST A POINT OF VIEW

Editors:

A. W. Gifford
Jennifer L. Gifford

P.O. Box 811
Ortonville, MI 48462

www.betenoiremagazine.com

Bête Noire is published by Dark Opus Press a division of Charm Noir Omnimedia P.O Box 811, Ortonville, MI 48062

ISBN-13: 978-0692397633
ISBN-10: 0692397639

This collection is a work of fiction. Names, characters, places, and scenarios are the products of the authors' imagination. Any resemblance to actual persons living or dead, places, or events is purely coincidental.

Bête Noire Magazine © 2015 Charm Noir Omnimedia

Cover art © 2015 A. W. Gifford

All stories, poems, artwork and photos © 2015 of their respective creators

All rights reserved. No portion of this publication can be reproduced by any means without the prior written permission from the authors of the work or Charm Noir Omnimedia

In This Issue

The Cold Girl

Jan McKeachie

When I was a little girl, I fell through the ice.

I shouldn't have. It was barely past New Year's, and any other year, the first thaw of spring wouldn't even have begun to reach our part of Maine. But the winter had been warm that year; the lake had frozen and thawed so many times that the ice was thin and tinted white by little bubbles of air. But even so, I should have been fine. It should have been enough to hold me. Except Nora's hick boyfriend had gotten a hunting rifle for Christmas, and the two of them couldn't think of anything funnier they could do with it than scare me while I was practicing my figure skating routine for the Valentine's Day Grand Prix.

To this day, I still honestly believe that they didn't mean to break the ice. Nora's boyfriend was just a bad shot. He'd never used the rifle before, wasn't ready for the way it kicked, so that when he squeezed the trigger, the shot went in the lake instead of into the woods at the shore.

I didn't have time to register what had happened as I came down from my toe loop. I hadn't even noticed they were there, hadn't heard them snickering over the sound of Tchaikovsky blaring from my headphones. All I understood was that when I started my jump, the ice under me was solid and milky-white, and when I finished it, little black cracks had snaked their way out in every direction from the spot where the bullet had hit.

I heard the sound of the shot, a single thunderclap that echoed inside my skull, punctuating every beat of the Tchaikovsky music like an enormous metronome.

I had time to see the flock of geese on the horizon take flight, frightened by the noise.

And then I looked down at my feet — by some happy miracle, the shot at least didn't hit *me* — and saw them twist and pop as they hit the surface of the ice. I screamed in pain and collapsed to all fours. My head hit the ice, and red lights flashed behind my eyes.

The ice cracked around me, booming, echoing over and over — the sound of the rifle going off.

Somewhere in the woods, unseen, Nora started screaming. I tried to climb to my feet.

"No, goddamn you!" Nora was saying, her voice competing with the clamor of Tchaikovsky and the still-echoing gunshot for room in my skull, "Stay where you are!"

But it was too late. As I brought myself to standing, the ice gave way under me.

And I fell through.

My iPod shorted out, and the music disappeared. In that silence, I couldn't even hear the blood pushing through my own veins. I faintly remember letting out a wordless scream as I realized what Nora had done. She'd killed me, I thought. There was no way she could get me out from under here.

But even the scream had no sound, down there under the ice. I felt bubbles against my face, big pockets of precious air that I'd released from my lungs and would never get back; as the bubbles drifted up away from my body, I couldn't hear them move, couldn't hear the *glug-glug-glug* that they should have made.

There was just that perfect, frozen silence.

The blackness.

The cold.

It took a long time for the cold to register. It didn't hit me at once, the way I would have expected it to. Instead, it slowly wrapped itself around me, an invisible anaconda trapping its prey under the surface, barely noticeable at first. And once it had me from my shoulders all the way down to my ankles, it started to squeeze.

I felt a pressure in my chest like I'd never felt before. What little breath I had left in my body trailed out of my nostrils, escaping towards the surface until there was nothing left in me.

But the pressure continued.

I remember thinking: Nora, I'm going to die like this.

And I'm not proud of what I thought next, because it wasn't anything noble or loving or forgiving. I didn't wish for Nora to have a happy life. I didn't ask God to look after my parents.

What I thought was: You bitch, I hope you feel terrible about this. I hope you're miserable for the rest of your life.

I opened my mouth and inhaled. Water flooded in through my nose, my mouth, making me choke and cough and squirm. But there was nothing I could do; the anaconda held me tight and wouldn't let me move.

The cold and silence and blackness that had surrounded me poured into my lungs and froze them over. Now I was cold and silent, too.

That was what it felt like to be dead.

What happens next is indistinct in my mind. There was motion, a current swirling against my cheek where there had been only stillness before. There was sound — someone was splashing above me, making noise that did not belong.

A pair of rough hands grabbed my wrist and jerked me towards the surface.

Another pair of hands — softer hands, kinder hands, hands belonging to the lake that had welcomed me into itself — reached up from below me and tried to drag me down.

I was suspended like that for an eternity.

And then the dead hands let me go.

I was pulled to the surface, to unwelcome warmth and light that burned against my skin. I wished so terribly in that moment that my savior had just left me under the ice and let me be dead. It was so much more peaceful down there.

But he didn't, of course. He pulled me to the shore and pushed down on my chest until I was forced to cough up every drop of the lake that had invaded my body.

Even after the water was gone, I felt cold.

I could still feel the anaconda slithering over my skin. Waiting for the right moment to start squeezing again.

"Are you okay, kid?" Nora asked. I retched and looked up at her.

"You killed me," I said. She grimaced, her lips pressing together into that ragged seam that always told me when she was upset.

"I'm sorry," she said, "Dear Jesus, I'm so sorry."

I was in no shape to walk, so Nora took me home in her boyfriend's pickup truck, even though the lake wasn't more than a mile away from our house. When she explained to our parents what had happened, Daddy went pale and poured himself a bourbon. Mom started yelling at Nora and didn't stop for the rest of her life.

They gave me Campbell's tomato soup, and told me it would warm up my insides.

It didn't.

I still felt cold.

When Mom and Daddy had gone out into the hall to argue about whether I should go to the hospital, Nora came and sat down by me and squeezed my hand.

"I didn't want to hurt you, kid," she said, "Honest. We were just having a little joke. You weren't supposed to go under like that."

This was the part where I was supposed to thaw up and remember how much I loved her. Forgive her. That was what I always did, wasn't it? When she cut my pigtails off in my sleep a week before the first day of school, I'd yelled at her for a while, but then I laughed it off and told her I liked my hair better that way — and then she'd let me practice French braiding on her, and we'd been sisters again.

But this time was different.

This time I'd slipped under the surface, been lost in a void far more frightening than any bad haircut.

Maybe it was because I was still numb, still frozen from the lake, but I couldn't bring myself to feel the love I was supposed to have for my sister. I couldn't even fake it. Instead, I turned away from her and took a long slurp of soup, the sucking sound filling up the silence between us.

"I feel terrible," Nora pleaded.

"Good," I said.

I didn't scream it, the way I would have any other time. I wasn't angry enough to scream. Instead, I hissed the word, just loud enough that I could be sure she would hear it, calculating the best way to hurt her. It caught her, squeezed her, made her go blue in the face. She jerked herself up to standing and tried to hold back a sob as she left the room.

I returned to my soup, my chattering teeth forcing my face into a cruel sort of smile.

Let her hurt, I thought, Just this once.

Late that night, after Nora had stopped sobbing in her bed, after Mom had turned out her reading light, popped a pill and rolled over for a night of unquiet sleep, the house fell silent. Truly silent, the way my lake had been.

My lake. Yes, I suppose I had started to think of it that way. It belonged to me and I belonged to it. We were the same, after all. Cold and dead.

I got out of bed and slithered down the hall. The light from the windows was eerie and distorted, as if the whole house had sunk under the sea.

Although the stairs were old and creaky every other day, that night, they accepted my weight silently and without protest, as if I wasn't there at all.

Outside, snow had begun to fall, thick and fast. By morning, it would be piled up in thick drifts over our driveway. Daddy would be late in to work.

The world was silent.

And then I saw a shape, standing out in the snow. It was hard to make out, blurred by snowflakes and somehow indistinct in and of itself. Every time I fixed my eyes on it, it shifted out of focus, like there was a pane of glass in between us that distorted my vision.

It raised a hand and waved to me, and I waved back.

It walked towards me, trudging through the snow, and as it drew nearer, I managed to make out that it was a little girl, about my age, with long black French braids coming down over her shoulders.

"Who are you?" I asked. My voice sounded so loud, so horribly loud, like a gunshot against the silence of the night. I scared an owl from its perch in the pine tree next to Daddy's car, and it flew out across the night, its *hoot-hoo* echoing through my bones.

The spell of silence was broken. I now heard the rustling of the trees, the sound of far-away traffic.

I looked for the little girl who had been standing in the snow, but she was gone.

I let out an explosive sigh. Suddenly aware that I was standing outside, barefoot, in mid-winter, I wrapped my bathrobe tighter around my waist. I tiptoed inside and crept back to bed as quietly as I could, but even so, the stairs creaked under me, and the door betrayed my passage with a loud *click*.

The next day, Mom took away Nora's driving license. Nora's face went tight, the way Daddy's did when he was upset, but she didn't say anything.

I didn't look up from my Raisin Bran. I knew I should feel bad for Nora. She had only been trying to give me a good scare. She never meant to put me in danger.

But there was a part of me, the cold part, that was glad to see her get punished like that.

I hope she's miserable, I thought, and as I did so, I felt a pleasant tightening in my chest that reminded me of the anaconda waiting under the ice.

That night, again, the house fell silent. I got out of bed, careful not to disturb the stillness a second time. I didn't want to restore the world to its normal state; I liked things better this way.

I thought to put on my snowboots before I stepped out onto the porch, lacing them up with the ease that comes from twelve long winters spent in New England. After a brief moment of thought, I also grabbed a jacket, gloves, and a scarf, bundling them around me to try to stay warm.

The girl was waiting for me again, in exactly the same spot. She gave me that same little wave, and then, without waiting to see what I would do, turned and started to march away through the snow, braids flapping behind her in the wind.

Naturally, I followed.

I didn't dare to speak, afraid that the sound of my voice would frighten her away again. Her feet didn't leave any marks in the snow, which in hindsight I suppose should have been a warning to me, but I didn't think anything of it. Hands shoved deep in the pockets of my bathrobe, eyes fixed on her shape as it disappeared into the woods, I ran after her. I breathed only through my nose, afraid that even the slightest sound would make my fairy playmate flee me forever.

My sense of time and distance was skewed, so that every shallow breath seemed to pass an hour and every step took me another mile into the forest. It wasn't long before I had no idea where I was — I had to rely completely on the girl to guide me through the woods.

She hid herself on the far side of a tree.

I quickened my pace to catch up with her, but she had disappeared.

Instead, I saw my house.

Two stories tall, with those old, chipped bricks around the porch and the bronze plaque on the front door that said *The Ford Family*, there was no way it could be any house but mine.

At the same time, there was no way it could be *here*, buried in the woods.

The sun was rising in the east.

The light hurt my eyes.

I went inside.

All the snowboots were gone from their place by the front door. They'd been replaced with flip-flops and sneakers.

The whole house was silent as I climbed the stairs. I'd gotten so used to the silence by now that I wasn't sure I remembered what noise was like, but I felt pretty sure that I found the silence preferable.

The door to the bathroom between my bedroom and Nora's was open.

Nora was standing at the sink, although it took me a moment to recognize her. She was *bigger* than the Nora I knew, not taller, but thicker — with wider hips and fuller breasts. More like a woman. Her face was tearstained and flushed red from stress; her lips were pursed together into that painful red line. In one hand, she clutched her cell phone to her ear; in the other, she was holding a pregnancy test.

I cowered back, afraid that she would see me and yell at me and tell me to get the hell away from her, the way she always did when she was angry and I got in her way. But she turned to look over her shoulder, looked straight at me, and didn't notice me.

That was when I understood that this wasn't really my house. It was a shadow, an illusion, something the little girl outside in the snow had wanted me to see.

Nora listened to her phone with her face all screwed up tight, and then threw it at the wall. It burst open, spilling its battery out onto the tile floor. She tried to scream, but no sound came out, as she descended on the phone and stomped on it with the heel of her shoe.

And then Nora Ford, my invincible older sister, slid to the floor and cried.

She cried for a long time, and I watched her. After a certain point, I came and wrapped my arms around her shoulders and wished I could tell her that everything would be okay, but she didn't feel my cold skin against hers. I tried to say something, to comfort her, but the oppressive silence of the house hushed my voice.

We lay together until she stopped crying, and for a minute, I thought she was going to be all right.

Of course she wasn't.

Silly me.

She went into Mom and Daddy's bedroom, a place that neither of us was ever, ever allowed to go. From the bedroom to the bathroom. To the medicine cabinet.

She pulled out a bottle of pills with a prescription made out to Mom for "insomnia as needed". And even as I understood what she was doing, as I tried to scream for her not to, she unscrewed the cap, tipped a handful of tablets into her palm, and started to swallow them.

One.

Two.

Three.

Four.

She kept going, mechanically popping them into her mouth, swallowing without chewing, without even making a face at the bitter taste.

I couldn't watch.

I looked away.

The whole thing had a dead, numb sort of feeling around it, like it wasn't totally real. Nora stumbled to her room and climbed onto her bed.

Was this going to happen? Was my sister going to die like this, curled up in a ball, crying herself to sleep for the last time? I hated the thought. I wished I'd never been dragged out of the lake, wished I'd just been left there where I never would have had to see this hideous future. I felt the cold part deep inside me throbbing, growing, sending little needles of ice out to my extremities and dulling my senses until all I felt was the cold.

Nora went still, her breath coming in shallow little gasps. My chest felt tight once again. The anaconda was squeezing.

I went back downstairs, back out into the woods outside the house. It was nighttime. The little girl with the French braids was there, waiting for me.

What was that? I tried to say, Who are you? Why did you bring me here?

But of course, I couldn't speak. My voice was gone. And the anger I should have felt at the death of my sister was replaced by a terrible, empty numbness.

As I drew near to her, the girl turned around and took off at a run. I chased her, swimming through the trees so fast that the forest around us became nothing but a great black blur.

I realized long before we stopped running where we were going. And sure enough, the girl came to a halt in the center of the lake, *my* lake, right over the spot where I'd plunged through the ice. A thin layer of new ice had reformed over the hole in the nights since I'd fallen, but it was fragile. Falling through again would be easy if I wasn't careful.

Why did you make me watch that? I tried to ask.

She didn't answer.

Uneasy, I stepped out onto the ice, balancing carefully to avoid slipping. One unsure step following another, I felt my way out into the center of the lake, until I was only standing five paces away from the other girl. She watched me the way a predator watches a wounded animal, and as I came closer to her, I finally saw her face. She was like me, terribly like me in every way, except for her eyes—those cold, dead eyes, with slits instead of pupils. A reptile's eyes.

The anaconda's eyes.

She held out a hand to me, but I pulled back, afraid.

Why did you make me watch my sister die?

She smiled, showed me the row of fangs she had instead of teeth, and winked.

And then I remembered the awful wish I'd made, when I was down there under the ice.

You bitch, I hope you feel terrible about this. I hope you're miserable for the rest of your life.

The girl—the anaconda—looked at me with her head tilted to one side.

You got your wish.

I thought about my sister, curled sobbing on the bathroom floor. About what would happen when my parents found her, how Daddy would go into his study and start drinking and call in sick for work the next morning. He'd refuse to tell anyone outside the family what had happened, would just say he had the flu and wanted to be left alone.

And Mom would stand there over Nora's body and scream at her, scream even though she was dead and wouldn't be able to hear, say how stupid she was, how selfish, and how *dare* she hurt her mother like that? Because that was what the women of my family always did. We yelled at each other when we cared.

I imagined the pain burning in Mom's face, and the last little breath of warmth that had been in me escaped out into the night. I felt cold and empty, dead for the second time.

Please, I thought, I don't ever want to see that again.

The girl extended her hand, and this time, I took it. It felt soft and dead, the same hand that had tried to hold me down in the lake when Nora's boyfriend had played the hero and swum down to save me.

I don't think I ever made it out from under the ice, though. Not really. Part of me, the cold part, still belonged to the lake and could never leave. I'd died down there, and I realized now that once I was dead—once the lake had taken me into itself—there could be no return to life. The lake would call me back, would always want me.

And what was waiting for me above the surface? Nora's death? My parents' agony? But down there, down in my lake, there was none of that. Only numbness. A beautiful, peaceful silence.

I like the silence so much better.

I stepped forward, crashed through the surface, sank back down into that nothingness. It was easier that way.

Nora killed herself about a year and a half after I went through the ice. Her boyfriend still comes by the lake every now and then. He cries and says nice things about her and drinks a beer to remember her.

He forgets that I'm down here.

By now, the lake and I are one. The water flows through me, cold and silent, and I don't know where I end and it begins.

Before my body was found, the fish used to nibble on my fingers and the end of my nose. Now, what was left of me has probably been buried in the cemetery on the edge of town. My limbs will be rotting away to nothing, festering and feeding a thousand grubs. But I don't mind.

I'm not really that little girl anymore.

I'm not really anything anymore.

But down here with me, swimming through the silence, is the anaconda, eternally waiting for someone to fall through the ice.

Ian McKeachie *was named a 2012 Davidson Fellow in literature for his portfolio, "Attitudes of Existence," which explored themes of suffering and loss in modern literature. He was born and raised in Reno, Nevada, but currently lives in the south of France. He has studied at l'Institut d'Études Politiques de Paris and at Columbia University in the City of New York. He speaks fluent French and Arabic, and has visited more than fifty countries worldwide. Ian has a short story slated for publication in the June 2015 issue of* Disturbed Digest.

The Howl 1856-2016

Marge Simon

"Who cowered in unshaven rooms in underwear ...

Henry Cook was a proud man, not one to cower.
It took a lot to get him down, yet having not a penny left,
sold his wife and son for a shilling at Croyden Market.
When that was spent, he sold his soul to Effingham.**

Bone crushing he could do and well, sucking marrow
from rotting bones, bashing those who dared to fight
for the freshest lot, and feared for being caught.
But on a day like any other, rooted to a wooden bench,
beating up those bones, he howled.

"who fell on their knees in hopeless cathedrals, ...

Oscar Wilde in Reading gaol, made to pay for sodomy,
broken dreams of decadence, blue china, golden rings,
embalmed in the darkness of Cellblock C,
a last psalm to a lover, his howl in silence sealed.

"I saw the best minds of my generation destroyed by madness ...

Kerouac's streaming lines, open spaces closing in,
Morrison on a high in Paris, springtime and heroin,
Basquait spraying boxcars with mischievous mystique,
lost their voices on the dark side of the sun.

"where the faculties of the skull no longer admit the worms of the senses ...

See the young men come and go, unaware of Michelangelo,
they're banging on the neighbor's door, thinking less and wanting more.
Outside, the coyote howls, caught in the maze of the city lights below.
He's starving, out of room and out of time, and he's not afraid of you.

*lines from Ginsberg's "Howl"
Effingham Workhouse, one of many, where the howl began three
centuries ago --
the workhouse howl, when no fight is left in a man, and nothing's to
be done about it.

Marge Simon's *works appear in publications such as* Strange Horizons,
Niteblade, DailySF Magazine, Pedestal Magazine, Dreams & Night-
mares. *She edits a column for the HWA Newsletter and serves as Chair of
the Board of Trustees. She has won the Strange Horizons Readers Choice
Award, the Bram Stoker Award™(2008, 2012, 2013), the Rhysling Award
and the Dwarf Stars Award. Collections:* Like Birds in the Rain, Unearthly
Delights, The Mad Hattery, Vampires, Zombies & Wanton Souls, *and*
Dangerous Dreams. Member HWA, SFWA, SFPA. *www.margesimon.com*

Many Lands I Have Travelled

N. L. Sakks

Every planet has one. A pin-hole. A portal. One spot, that is neither atmosphere, nor solid matter, but a knot of raw energy. Once you spot one, that's it. You are aware of them all. The signs. Subtle shifts in the atmosphere's pressure, that slight tingling that you feel in your hand. All reveals itself to you, so that you now see what was always there. No longer are you ignorant. And when you find one, when you touch it, it pulls you in, and it spits you out, in a land, that is new and foreign.

Years ago, I came across my first portal.

Mine was a land that was bare and untried. There were no trials for our kind. We did not struggle against the elements. It was a planet without much beauty. Without the turn of seasons, where the lands offered food, in little variety. We lived off of what the lands provided. Mostly, red fruit, from the barest of trees, its skin tough; its taste sour. It would stain our clothing. The sky, always grey; the air warm and not quite humid. We kept quiet, because there was never much to speak about. We all looked the same, now that I think back to it. It may have been the dust in the air, sticking to us and to our clothing. The soft winds, which swept over all. Steady and constant not quite disturbing, but always there. All our garb, worn away and dirty, like the lands. We did not grow fat, as many do in other worlds, where food is plenty. We were thin and tall, our kind. We were not happy, but of this we were not aware. We did not fight, we did not hate, we did not love passionately and we did not face hardship.

They knew about portals on my second planet. They saw me come out of the portal. They all knew about it, and no one so much as commented. Ressources there were plenty, and I was not without. But I'd seen another world now. Another land. And I could not help myself. I wanted something more. It's strange. That you can have nothing, and want for nothing, and that when you catch a glimpse of something new and flashy, you forget how to be content.

Why did they only look at me with disinterest? I thought. *Were they not curious?* I should have made myself humble. I should have asked about the portals. But I kept to myself. I assimilated, until I found the next portal, another outgoing portal, and then again I left. And when someone finally told me. When I finally found out, it was already too late.

"Man is a fragile creature", he told me. "He is but bones, and tissue, and flesh, and fragile at that. He can not think to trespass on time and what we know as space. Fickle is he who thinks himself above those constraints which define natural law. A man cannot come in and out and go as he may. For we were not made as such."

A man told me this. And it did not even matter to me. Nothing really compared to that second world at this point. Fifteen portals I had travelled. If only I could have come across something like what I'd been brought to by the first portal. I've seen places of war. I've seen the harshest of elements, where a man cannot stay outside long, without running for cover. Worlds where there is evil in the people, a blankness in their eyes, so that you can't help but feel sorry for them. And you can't help but feel that they would like to hurt you and feel it would somehow better themselves. It's all barren, I thought. In all these places, in all these lands there's really nothing here.

"Greedy", he called me. The old man, who told me about the portals. He was tall, and lean, and slightly hunched over. His skin, looked weathered, all the fat, gone away from it. He had the palest of eyes. Blue eyes. They were young eyes, I thought. Which was a strange thought, because by all indication, the man was old.

But it made sense.

That impression I had of him, it made sense.

He spoke to me, and I only partly listened, until he leaned in, and said "I've travelled many portals too, my friend."

In all my travels, I searched, I looked, until I found what I was looking for. That charge in the air, that weird line of tension. I told no one of my purpose. No one of my search, for a world, somehow, better than my own.

The man knew. Something about the look of me drew him in. As if the portals had done something to me. Something this man could see.

"Don't go back", he told me. And I knew he meant for me to stay away from the portals. His eyes fixed on me. That weird shade of blue, or pale grey. He shook his head slowly, and then he told me his age. And I understood. I understood why the old man had somehow appeared young to me. That he was not really old at all. And I understood about portals. About what they do to a body. How it ages someone ahead of their time. I understood that time, really was not mine. And I think that the process may have already started. I feel different. Not weak, but used up somehow. And I think that for me, it may already be too late.

N. L. Sakks *is a PhD student in biology. While her daily activities are firmly rooted in fact, she is especially partial to the world of fiction. She previously won a short story contest for her piece titled "Dreaming" and her short story "Southern Road" was published in Bosley Gravel's* Cavalcade of Terror.

MAN WITH A GUN *by Alfred Klosterman*

Alfred Klosterman *lives in Philadelphia and has long worked as a graphic artist for printing firms. He's read and collected fantasy and science fiction most of his life. He has contributed artwork to many genre small press publications for many years. These include* Cemetary Dance, The Horror Show, Eldritch Tales, Space & Time *and* Dark Horizons. *He's devoted to black & white work, inspired by the many fine illustrators he's enjoyed in vintage magazines. Other interests include gardening, pets and really loud music.*

RAVINGS

Mohammad Saif Al-Wahedi

What devilish, demonic rituals our ancestors endorsed themselves in I dare not articulate; yet I have seen a he twenty-first of December which have fully quenched my thirst for any such relevant knowledge. There is peace of mind in ignorance; in the unawareness of the horrors perpetuated through history. In my case, however, I have been enlightened with a horrible truth whose eldritch nature awakens nightmares whenever the moon, fully round, shines. My own fragile peace of mind has been preserved only through the tiny, flickering hope in which the occurrence on the twenty-first could have been nothing but the ravings of a drunkard. It is of note to say that on that particular day I was as sober as a judge.

The reader must surely have seen, or at least heard, about the standing stones of Stonehenge. They stand in the South West of England, sprawled in an area called Amesbury. I will not drawl behind the fact that these primordial stones were erected in the Neolithic Ages by the mysterious peoples of that time. There is an infamous, lesser-known monolith known as Woodhenge by the woods of Amesbury, only a couple of miles away from Stonehenge. This sacrificial henge was discovered in 1925 by one Alexander Keiller, and since then has been the subject of numerous studies and excavations. I have been involved with the latter, and this is where the twist betwixt the two comes into place.

Pardon the unseemly preamble. An introduction is in order. I am Doctor Neville Hastings of the Royal Archaeological Society.

In my childhood years I've lived in the countryside of Amesbury, in a small, homely cottage just around the corner from Woodhenge; separated only by a Catholic chapel and a stale meadow whose shrubs reeked with field rodents. And whenever I am in a vacant mood, I would abandon whatever inane occupation I have got my hands on and swing by Woodhenge. I would then keep gazing for what seems like eternity, mesmerized by the ancient relics whose purposes are still to this day unknown.

From time to time, a commotion made by visitors visiting Woodhenge — varying from students, researchers and tourists — would block the single-way lane up the road. On these few, occasional days, I would even be nosier than usual, barging into whatever that was being done. And depending wholly on the amicability of the visitors, I would either be gently rebuffed or given a simplistic explanation of what was being done, which, to be frank, I understood nothing of. And time passed…

There is no need to delve into trivial details, as I just find myself straying away from the subject whose essence I wish to convey. A couple of months ago, spurred on by memories of childhood, I have proposed before my colleagues in the Royal Archaeological Society a deeper, much more extensive study into Woodhenge, for I believed that the wooden pillars could not have been created purposelessly. My proposal was approved, and I started working on the spot. And what is the date that I have chosen? Yes, the twenty-first of December.

It was windy. The ground was covered in a white blanket of snow, and with the sun locked in the middle of the sky, its fires giving off a reddish, subdued light — just like dying embers — made quite the melancholy scene. Coughing audibly, I parked the car in front of the gate to Woodhenge. I then fished out my equipment, consisting mainly of a photovoltaic lamp — which charges its battery by capturing sunlight during day — food and a shovel (for exploring purposes). The wind was roaring, and brittle flakes of ice were broken and scattered everywhere, blurring vision. I attempted to warm my hands by rubbing them vigorously, yet to no avail. I even considered turning back all the way home, yet I meant business; and business was to be done.

The snow crunched beneath my feet as I trod over it, its sound like the peal of crushed bones. Unlatching the lock, I opened the gate and walked into the henge. Taking in the beauty of my surroundings, my eyes took in the symmetrical wooden pillars, the tall grass, the trees and the huge circle the wooden pillars made in the centre of the henge. I fished out my paper pad and started taking notes.

And then I saw it. A mound that was noticeably higher than any surrounding terrain. It was in the very centre of the henge. Looking around me, I brought forth my shovel. I hauled dirt and threw it aside. I kept shoveling off dirt until I confirmed my suspicions. A skull grinned at me toothlessly. Its hair still stuck in grizzled patches to its temple, but was in such a state of decay that I averted my eyes in disgust. This special placement of this corpse meant only one thing: that it was part of a ritual. A nebulous, disgusting abomination of a ritual.

Placing my notebook beside me, I crouched and squinted at the skull. The sun was dying behind the hills, its dying light giving off a weak, useless radiance. The cranium, which I handled with great care, was very petite and diminutive, as if belonging to a child. It was intact, that is except for the sawed-off edges that were worn off by time. The parietal and suture regions of the skull were shorter than normal, giving the facial features an apish, bestial quality, which confirms the theories in which ancestors had smaller brains with more limited capacities.

There in the naked wilderness, with the freezing wind lashing at my face, a sense of total stuporous drowsiness; more sensual than physical, washed over my senses. It was like the mist in the air, dampening my senses and distorting reality. I buried the skull in its sepulcher, and standing up, went over to a naked fir tree, where I rested my head against the cold bark. *Only a moment,* I said, *just to rest.*

The sun well-nigh vanished, and the land, once silhouetted only in certain patches, became one seamless shadow again. I fumbled in the darkness for the lamp and turned it on. The illumination was feeble, yet capable enough of throwing shadows everywhere. I hugged the lamp for warmth…and slept.

Whether that sleep was induced due to physical exertion (though I didn't do much) or the numbing coldness I do not know, yet I have developed in my mind far more terrible explanations whose incomprehensible nature forbids me to tell. Nevertheless, be it sleep or incantations, I am ashamed of my siesta, and its occurrence was in the most critical time.

I woke with blasphemous chants of the wind echoing in the henge. Still bleary from awakening, I beheld before me a misty landscape, where everything was swathed in a veil of pellucid translucency. The lamp was long since dead. I attempted to stand. Just as my feet were about to take my weight, some force crippled it and I fell on the ground again. My hands I no longer felt, and I am sure that had light been there, they would have looked blue and lifeless. Terror seized me in its merciless grasp, rendering me handicapped in both body and mind.

The tempo of the chants increased, and with it the wind's ferocity positively complied. And then out of the entombed earth they came. Ghostly apparitions, resembling humanoid figures clad in furs and padded leather. They shone with their own iridescence, yet that radiance did not extend to the surrounding objects beside them, thus still maintaining the clutch of the mist on the land. The phantasms floated in the air and commenced dancing in a weird manner, all the while flavoring their dance with words from another tongue in a language which bore a great resemblance to English, but which was more inclined towards German barbarity of pronunciation.

All of the latter I watched with great perplexity and disbelief. Had I not been paralysed in fear, I would have uttered the most unmanly scream my parched throat could muster. Yet alas, I watched this grotesque theatrical show, the dirty ground my seat, the gnarled rough wood my cushion, and the cold dead lamp my popcorn bowl. I watched helplessly, as spineless as the denizens who see their countries wreaked into havoc but are powerless to interfere.

The wind drowned whatever horrible spells the poltergeists uttered. They stood in a circle whose centre was occupied with a small child tied to the central wooden pillar in the henge. The child, be it a he or a she, (for it was indiscernible in the dark) was as naked as its birthday, that is except for a lousily-worn rag around its waist. It cried in vulnerability as the specters chanted maniacally around it. Finally, one of the figures, whose stature and build identified him as a male, strode forward and pulled a hood over his face. I caught a fleeting flash of metal, and gasped in horror as realization struck me. It was a sacrificial knife, rough at the edges and blunt. The hooded figure stood in front of the child. Crying loudly, he slit the youngster's throat in one quick slash and filled a small wooden bowl with the gushing fountain of blood. The child quivered as his soul bled away with his blood one last time and ceased to move.

The eidolons then added oil to the blood and lit the ghastly concoction ablaze. They left it at the feet of the young child, where the conflagration quickly engulfed his (or her) skin in flames. The figures stood motionless around, watching with interest, as if the scene before them was not the result of their actions. The sky rumbled loudly, as if some metaphysical deity was appeased by the massacre. The figures prayed...

And so did I. *O Merciful Lord,* I said, *protect me in my hour of need. Bless me with a painless death whose swiftness is none other than a mercy from You... Let me die 'fore my death is pronounced with that kni...* And with these ravings in mind, I found myself unconscious, adrift and free. I embraced that sleep, for I thought that it was the lethargy of death.

Next day, I woke up to find myself in the same awkward position as before. My back felt as stiff as the tree I slept on. The sun was shining high in the sky, and its warmth gave me energy to go on. Some life returned to my hands and feet, no doubt due to the warmth. Standing up, I waited for my sleepy thighs to regain balance before moving on. The wind—formerly a maelstrom—now became a gentle breeze. I limped and hobbled all the way to my car. Oh, my beloved car! Settling in comfortably into the leathery, soft seat I turned on the heating system and drove off. With one last glance, I looked at the henge—that terrible, monstrous origin of all that is barbarous—and sped off the one-way lane.

The following day, emboldened with companionship, I told my colleagues that they ought to accompany me to Woodhenge for one last visit. *Why* and *what* I did not answer, but told them to escort me nevertheless. Entering again into the malicious place again, I did one thing only. I strode purposefully to the centre of the henge, where that accursed mound once stood, with my associates tailing me. The shovel was still where I lift it on the twenty-first, with its shaft halfway buried in the ground. I hauled dirt off until I unmasked the skull beneath. Groaning in disgust, my comrades averted their eyes away in repulsion. In that moment, with my friends' attention scattered, I swear in God's name thrice that the skull *somehow* turned itself to my direction and *grinned*.

We left everything as it was and ran. Whatever occurred on the twenty-first of December; the night of the Winter Solstice, I don't know and don't *want* to know. However, I know that I won't *ever again* tread a foot, or even cross paths, with the accursed woods of Woodhenge.

Mohammad S. Al-Wahedi *was born in 1998. He displayed a keen inter-est in creative writing, especially after being "stimulated" by short stories from the progenitor of the weird genre, H.P. Lovecraft. He lives in Abu Dha-bi, the capital of the United Arab Emirates. Al-Wahedi has also published a collection of short horror stories titled* "Memorabilia of the Horror & Oth-er Tales of Terror". *His goal was to see his writings published.*

Another Light

Wesley D. Gray

The echoing haunt
of breaking waves
cringe upon the verge
of this world
and the next,
rising to the tower,

white stone bleached
from wind and sea and salt,
into the eye
whose light reaches
cresting depths
where Lost Ones lie
in dripping graves,
to fill saddened ears
dwelling upon the loss.

And when Moon staggers in,
wipes her feet upon the mat,
another light is seen
at aberrant angles
from the rocks,
finding form
in lamenting figure,

bleeding, glowing,
bleeding, glowing—
searching for home.

*Wesley D. Gray is a writer, an author of fiction, and a self-proclaimed poet.
His chapbook,* Come Fly with Death: Poems Inspired by the Artwork of
Zdzislaw Beksinski *is available now. If you're ready to delve deeper, be sure
to visit his blog,* Marrowroot.com.

The Shark Cult of Launasi Lagoon

William Akin

The distant drums are constant, metering out the time Winston has left. He can't put the circumstances of his life together, can't make sense of how he came to be hiding in this cave from the headhunters. He knows it is a waste of precious seconds to worry about the past rather than deal with the present but his mind is scattered. It clings to each little notion or fancy that passes through. When he closes his eyes the cave and the jungle outside fade away and images march through his head, some old and some new. They come and go as they please and carry him away with them.

He sees the bay and the priest with an obsidian knife. He can hear the screeching pig as the blade slides across its throat. A purple flower blooms and swells beneath the azure water as the animal falls silent, then still. He sees the shark fins rolling in, the black and gray sails of some menacing armada. The priest continues the ceremony, offering the other three swine tied up along the edge of the dais. They kick and fight to the very end. His hands plunge beneath the water, deep into the swirl of blood and teeth yet he is unharmed, rewarded by his gods and faith.

Winston's thoughts return to the cave and the half-circle of the dying pink sun. Had he blinked or had he fallen asleep? Had a second passed, or a minute? An hour or a week? How long before the drums quicken their pace? Time is slipping away from him. Where is it going? Where did time come from to begin with? Why the hell is he even thinking such nonsense?

They had poisoned him, damn it.

He tries to fight the priest's brew and focus on the situation at hand. The elixir is warping his mind but he knows he must concentrate. He's a wounded bird, flightless and far from home, and the hounds are about to be let loose.

Run, Winston urges himself.

Why? Winston asks.

Headhunters. Run.

Where?

To the dinghy. Yes, towards the south side of the island, two miles off shore. That is if they have yet to find it stowed there, of course.

It's still there, a third Winston chimed in. *You might, just might, live through this after all.*

Really? The sound of the drums grows louder and bolder as other hands join the circle down in the village.

Really. If you just keep your head about you, Winston assures himself, chuckling out loud. He imagines himself sipping gin back at the club in London. He lights his pipe and crosses his legs, building the suspense of his tale of escape from the tribe of headhunters. "And I said to myself, I said, Winston old top, you must keep your head about you. The boys all harrumph and guffaw in stodgy delight."

The scene sends Winston laughing even harder. He sees his body doffing his head as if it were a hat, the two separating like some drawing from a child's book. They bid each other a fond and polite adieu, having decided to go off on their own paths. He sees his skull, stacked among a hundred others in a longhouse, the skulls of generations of priests and kings. They gossip through the night, a cacophony of cackling and hollow voices that becomes a chorus of chattering teeth on cold Pacific mornings. He sees his head shrunken, a sixth adornment to hang about the neck of the priest. His skin is tanned and taut, his muttonchops and thinning hair meticulously preserved. His tiny face is still howling at his own joke and the other five heads on the strand stare back at him as if he were a raving lunatic.

Perhaps they are right and he has gone mad. Look at him, rolling around in the cool dirt in fits of hysterics, stitched up with a grin so wide and persistent it pains his face. His sides ache and burn as if pierced and he gasps for breath.

A monkey or a parrot or a demon screeches off in the jungle, cutting at once through his mirth. His heart stops and his stomach plunges. He tries to laugh it away but the laughter is all gone now, replaced by a nibbling then gnawing fear. The entire world outside the cave is peering in, watching him. The walls and dark shadows around him are watching too, as they bleed and slither at the edge of his vision. He is alone, separated from every thing that exists outside him, and every thing that exists outside him is observing and poised to strike.

He is sweat-soaked and exhausted, waiting for death in a damned hole. *It is the priest's potion,* he tells himself, over and over again. It propels him through these dreamy worlds, from roaring bliss to utter fear in an instant. His reality has been bent to their accord and his unease.

For the six days following the sacrifice in the bay, Winston was kept locked in a small hut under constant guard. His comforts were meager but identical to those afforded his captors. The first three days he was given fish, prawn and lemongrass soup, fresh fruit, and coconut water. In the evenings he was presented with a gourd of a strong and sweet distillation, much like rum, but cloudy and richer.

On those drunken evenings he studied his plight. Would he share the same fate as his men or something even worse? In his intoxication he imagined catching the guards sleeping, and slipping away from his thatched cell unnoticed. He would make his way toward the southern shore and swim against the high tide surf to that thin and tenuous sandbar where the dinghy waited like a hopeful child. Even in his fantasies, though, dark shadows loomed above and hovered beneath him. Even the joy of drunkenness was adorned with fear as his nascent happiness eroded away in perpetual cycles of birth and death.

On the fourth and fifth days he was not given food at all, only a small bowl of fresh water to drink. His mood turned dark and the nights were sleepless. His days were spent trying to reckon what this change might mean, trying to read some sign of the future in the cool water as if it were a scrying glass.

Winston didn't believe he was the same sort of man his four crewman had been. He wasn't a rapist nor was he a thief, though in the drunken dereliction of his duties he was, perhaps, even worse. He had turned a blind eye to their deeds, ignored each of their transgressions against the islanders until it had been too late. If theirs had been a cult of sin then Winston must have surely been the presiding priest. If theirs had been a murderous tribe then Winston must have surely been the chieftain. Through two long nights of toss-turning judgment of himself, he found no justification for his own pleas of mercy.

On the sixth day he was given neither food nor water. Instead the guards left him with a small wooden cage. Inside the cage was a kestrel, its muddy brown and black wings clipped so short they might as well have been removed. Not too promising as far as omens go, he concluded.

The kestrel's squawking woke him early on the seventh morning. Winston could hear the shuffling of bare feet on sand and the chiming of shell jewelry, the whispers and murmurs of a small crowd, a tidal swell washing up towards the door of his hut. The guards entered and bound his hands behind him with thick seaweed ropes then led him outside and into the sun, for the first time in a week. The priest waited, flanked by his attendant and another man bearing a drum. Behind them stood a group of ten very young men and a filthy black cur. The dog was leashed but snarling and frothing at the mouth and something in its eyes matched the moods of those young warriors.

The acolyte retrieved the cage and passed it to the priest. He removed the struggling falcon and thrust it out towards Winston, uttering a single word. The drummer took up a slow beat and the priest tossed the confused bird to the ground. It hopped off across the clearing, towards the edge of the forest. The priest turned his back on the kestrel and stared into Winston's eyes. The drum beat on and the dog whined and growled behind them.

The mutt's tail drooped between its legs and its head sank low as the tall man and his necklace of shrunken heads approached. He took the animal's leash and spoke another word, this time directed towards the young warriors. The tempo of the drum doubled as he released the hound. It shot forward, arcing off in frenzied chase, an arrow in flight, piercing the ferns and vines as it disappeared into the trees. The priest stared at the young men. The only sound or movement came from the drummers hands across the goatskin. From somewhere closer than Winston would have imagined, came the screech of the kestrel.

The priest repeated the first word he had spoken and pointed again at Winston, who was less and less certain now that it meant "bird." He repeated the second word, most likely not "dog," and indicated the young men with a flourishing wave.

Well, I must say, he does have a way with a lack of words, Winston thought, finding strange comfort in this new twist of fate. Death stalks us, each and every moment of each and every day, following just behind us or waiting around the next corner, it is true, but that is a subtle sort of dying, one often easy to ignore. This, however, was immediate and visceral, undeniable and irrefutable. He was to run and they were to hunt him. He might make it to the sandbar, to the dinghy, then maybe all the way up to Auki, come sunrise. He just as well might die. He might lose his head, might have his body fed to sharks until all that remained were chewed bones strewn among the shipwreck debris littering the bottom of the lagoon.

The priest led the group deeper into the jungle. Winston studied the shadows of his captors and the position of the sun as they walked, calculating their approximate location in his head with each step, a pleading prayer of refuge from a condemned man.

The men halted at the edge of a clearing. The acolyte ran ahead of them, the crushed seashell path crunching beneath his bare feet. One of the guards withdrew a flint knife and walked around Winston while the other stood chest to chest with him and muttered a few phrases in a tone meant to intimidate. The first man cut loose his bonds and pushed him towards the priest, who beckoned him to follow. Winston's heart was leaping from his ribcage, attempting to flee of its own volition before being evicted by some sort of ceremonial force. He stepped forward with his head held high and proper though, determined not to meet this summons as a quarry-slave, not to be scourged by any dungeon or thatched hut.

An earthen pot hung over a low fire in the center of the hand cleared circle. Grass mats were arranged at precise intervals around the pot and next to each was a deep gourd-bowl. The priest led Winston to one of the mats while the young men took their places.

The holy man stood outside the circle and walked around its circumference. He began a low and melodious chant, almost a song to Winston's ears. He passed from man to man, anointing their foreheads and faces with deep umber smears of something that felt cool and comforting.

He continued circling the group. In his left hand he carried a human skull draped with shark's teeth on hempen ropes and mounted on a short staff. He flicked it back and forth, left then right, a percussive rattle to underscore his chanting. The song seemed to be in a different language, using tones and pitches Winston had never heard these people use. There was nothing in any human language he had ever heard that sounded as soft and soothing as this song, formed from notes so loose they seemed to be only half-sounds, not fully born into space yet somehow audible.

The acolyte filled a nautilus shell from the pot. He approached the man on Winston's left and lifted the shell above his head. The man held his breath and the acolyte poured the sludgy brew into his mouth. He turned towards Winston next, again holding the potion aloft as if making an offering or seeking a blessing. Winston opened his mouth and closed his eyes. The liquid was as thick and black as tar and tasted sharp and bitter. He gagged but forced himself to keep it down, a child accepting his castor oil, just as every other man in the circle did in his own turn.

Afterwards, some of the men chanted or muttered beneath their breath but most sat in silence. Winston's stomach began to ache, a dull spark at first but soon spreading into a sickening blaze. He wretched and heaved and realized why the gourds had been placed at their sides. The young warriors were all vomiting too, groaning and wailing and clutching their bellies. The man to Winston's right looked pale and afraid. He shouted something and then fell face forward onto his mat. All around the circle, men were losing consciousness and tumbling to the ground. Like trees cut down to become mighty canoes, Winston thought, just before his own mind swooned into the rushing darkness.

When he became aware again, it was black, pitch black, and icy cold, and he must have died because he was not breathing and it no longer seemed to matter. He moved through the darkness, getting nowhere, bumping into things from time to time, perhaps the ghosts of the young warriors, lost too, in this dark purgatory. For a long time there was nothing but cold and darkness and glancing bumps in the infinite night, nothing but nothingness.

At some point, he had the thought of taking a breath again. He had the deep urge to do so, as if he had been holding his breath all through that long, cold night. He crawled through the darkness, along an instinctual course, until he could see a faint shimmer of light. He struggled towards the dim blue glow, swimming up from the ocean bottom and into the sunlight.

Perhaps, Winston thought, they have killed me and tossed my corpse into the deep trench alongside the reef and at last my spirit is rising to heaven despite the sins of my body.

Then the ancient tortoise that once had been the man called Winston breeched the ocean's surface. The sun was bright and high above a rolling and endless sea. There was no land in sight and the very concept of land slipped from his mind as he swam through the furious waves. Cresting a whitecap, he could see, off in the distance, a hole floating upon a single calm spot. The hole looked very much like a window or perhaps a mirror but as soon as those words had entered the tortoise's mind they melted away and no longer had meaning to him. He could see palm trees and a fire and sleeping men through the sea-tossed hole, but then these things too, all lost their meaning. The tortoise dove back beneath the sea, to the sanctuary of the murky and stiller depths below.

And then there was darkness, coldness, darkness, for maybe a hundred years before another breath was drawn from the air above the endless ocean.

How many cycles passed this way without change will never be known, tortoises understand nothing of the nature of numbers or counting. Even if one existed that might possess such faculties, no creature has ever lived upon the earth or below the sea with the ability to measure the sorts of infinities the situation would have required. Countless is as close as we may ever come.

Then, once again, instinct drew the creature up towards the bright torch of the sun, just as it had done those many, many, instances before. This time though, circumstance and serendipity aligned in a curious display of luck. The long forgotten hole floated just above his head, filled with strange shapes and colors that guided him onward. The tortoise swam faster, pointing its nose into the center of the circle and slipping its head inside, as the head of an ox is placed into a wooden yoke.

Winton could smell the dying embers of the fire. He opened his eyes and sat up. A tall figure approached. It looked like the priest but his form was distorted, a gaunt reflection from a funhouse mirror that faded out and trailed off at the edges. The five shrunken heads he wore were screaming, tortured souls with faces writhing in agonizing contusions, wailing for justice and release. The young warriors were beginning to stir from their own strange dreams. The priest helped him to his feet and placed a leather braid, strung with the severed head of the kestrel, around his neck. The man spoke the word that didn't mean "bird" and shoved Winston towards the jungle's edge just as the slow rhythm of the drums began to roll up the hills, a rising thunder from the village below.

Judging from the angle of the sun as it slips into its orange shroud and fills the mouth of the cave, that must have all been an hour or two ago. It's still hard to tell for certain. His head is dancing with pictures and memories, stray thoughts and odd sounds, and a thousand colors or more. Winston struggles to put them aside, to accept them for the trivialities they are and formulate a plan. Two miles to the south, the dinghy is waiting, if it had not been discovered yet. He tries to bring it into clearer focus but the images of a dozen other boats he has rowed rush in to take its place.

The world is spinning fast, all around and underneath him. He manages to leash his mind long enough to determine the general direction of the southern shore. A perfunctory prayer slips from his heart and lips as he strikes out into the jungle. He wonders if it had been god or fate or its own strength that had freed the tortoise. Winston decides he trusts god and fate about the same, and he isn't willing to gamble on either. Instead he sprints headlong upon his self-chosen path, intent and clumsy.

Running quickens his blood and the hallucinogen courses through his veins with a new vigor, gripping him even tighter. He sees the bay and the priest with an obsidian knife, can hear his crewmen grunting and squealing as, one by one, the blade slides across their throats. He can hear the slap and splash of the feeding frenzy as the sharks rip and tear at their gurgling remains. He can see the chunks of flesh and strands of entrails swirling like dark clouds in the sky blue water. Their heads and skulls not even deemed fit for trophies but better left to sink below to the cowards and scavengers crawling through the mud and waiting their turns to feed, forever purging the island of their crimes.

The jungle whisks by, brushing at his shoulders and swiping at his face. He has the sensation of running in place while the forest is rushing ahead then circling back to pass him again. He is getting nowhere, bewitched or enthralled by the wicked glamour of the priest. Winston can see him still, smiling down on the scene, standing as tall as the trees ahead and still chanting. The five heads strung around his giant neck are no longer shrunken and the anguish crawling across their faces is even more clear and frightening.

Reality is falling down around him now. Sharks swim through his mind and kestrels wing through his thoughts. The froth-dripping teeth of rabid dogs nip at his heels and a score or more dinghies row off into the sunset. Winston keeps running, running past mirrors and over oceans, running through houses heaped with fresh and ancient bones, running into the steady sea breeze that whispers in his ears.

He stops at the edge of a cliff overlooking the ocean, the entire world seeming to pause along with him. All of the things in his head cease and the sounds of the drums fade to silence. Everything around him stops, as if he had sidestepped out of the stream of time and found a sacred space between the seconds.

The scraps of the day are swallowed by the sea and a green ray flashes up into the heavens, lingering for a moment before it fades into the new born night. A stillness remains in its wake. The stars are bright and rising, woven together with tracers of light in a great jeweled net that someone's god has cast across the world, snaring them all.

The drums return, fierce and faster now, his heart matching the rhythm. The dogs must be loose by now, sniffing out his trail. He runs on, determined to earn whatever might await him beyond this, beyond tonight, beyond life, beyond even death, perhaps.

His feet are raw and bleeding and he stumbles often. Parrots screech and shoot up through the trees in his wake, flares giving away his every move. A spear thwocks into a tree beside him, driving his feet even faster. He weaves off the trail and dives into the underbrush, concentrating on his pulse and gasping breath, willing them to slacken and stifle. Feet shuffle and spears rattle above as he tries to shrink into the ferns. The hunters pass and war cries sound in the distance.

The hallucinations are fading, replaced with recurring déjà vu, a knowingness and familiarity with his surroundings, something animal and instinctual that leads him on. He slides down the hillside and finds a small creek seeking the sea with an urgency that rivals his own.

Winston takes to the stream, ankle deep, warm and powerful. It flows into a small canyon filled with the scent of the nearby ocean. A war cry sounds from atop the high stone wall on his left and another responds from the right, the pack closing in. He races toward the opposite end of the canyon, arrows raining down around him.

The creek escapes the encroaching walls in a high pressure blast and twenty foot fall, a fact Winston realizes in the same moment he decides to leap anyway. He strikes the bottom of the shallow pool beneath hard enough to sprain a wrist and crack a few ribs.

Far past the clarity and peace he had found just moments earlier, he still manages on along the rocky path, down the tumbling cliff side, towards the cove hidden below. The cries of the warriors are drawing closer and closer and the drums are frenetic, drowning out even the sound of the surf.

The white sand is cool beneath his feet. A man sits watching the waves roll out. He stands and draws his bow. A childhood memory sparks in Winston, of watching a travelling magician catch an arrow in midflight by smacking it between his open palms. It seems, right here and now at least, to be an easy thing to do. Which it isn't of course, not at all, but the archer lets loose a clumsy shot, so stunned that the target is still charging towards him. The flint point glances off Winston's cheek while his empty hands clap together as if in delight.

He tackles the man. The boy, he realizes. Not a warrior, not a dog, just a skinny pup. The pup wriggles beneath him, brandishing a coral knife. Winston wrenches it from his hand and presses it close to the pup's throat. He thinks of the pigs, of the kestrel, and the tortoise too. He tosses the child's knife into the ocean and breaks the bow over his knee.

His face flushes then falls slack and numb. Some new poison from the pup's arrowhead, he assumes. The warriors are growling and screaming as they break free of the jungle and skitter up the strand. The moon is high and bright and long shadows twist and ripple beneath the sea. He dives in and swims out, just a few miles short of salvation.

The water in the cove is icy and shallow, as clear as the empty space between you and me. The light of the moon casts away the darkness and reveals the shadows to be corpses, scores of floating corpses, anchored to the seabed. They shake and dance with pale and perfectly preserved faces, looking like the fathers and mothers of the warriors and the pup and even the priest. The ancestors, tucked away in the serenity of the white sand cove along the southernmost shore of a paradise he is leaving behind.

Winston swims, swims harder and faster than he ever has in his life. Just two miles, he tells himself. Just two miles, but the sea turns warmer with each passing stroke, and black shapes and gray sails are rushing into greet him.

William Akin *abides in the Pacific Northwest, perched on the edge of an extinct cinder cone, alongside his wife, two daughters, and a dog with which he has a rather ambivalent relationship. He hasn't a strong grasp on the differences between prose and poetry, nor myth and truth, often confusing them hopelessly.*

Traces of the Alchemist

Bruce Boston

are found lingering
in the accidental streets
and bizarre curio bazaars
of a tourist mecca.

Whispers of the magician
are heard echoing
in shadow enclaves
along the tracks
that lace the world.

Images of the hierophant
form and reform
in the roiling clouds
that follow the rush
of a winter storm.

Atoms of the avatar
reside in a fraction
of a fraction of the air
you breathe into your lungs.
Atmospherically there!

Traces of the alchemist
linger and inhabit
the accidental streets
and diminutive noir cafes
of a compelling dream.

Bruce Boston *is the author of more than fifty books and chapbooks, including the novels* The Guardener's Tale *and* Stained Glass Rain. *His writing has received the Bram Stoker Award, a Pushcart Prize, the Asimov's Readers Award, and the Grand Master Award of the Science Fiction Poetry Association.*

MISSION CONFIRM   *by Denny E. Marshall*

Denny E Marshall *has had art, poetry and fiction published, some recently.
To see more of his works visit his website at www.dennymarshall.com*

ORTHOGRAPHICAL TORMENT

J. J. Steinfeld

A twenty-one-year-old man, having recently graduated *magna cum laude* from university and about to begin next week his first full-time job with a large research institute, was walking toward a downtown bar to meet the older married woman with whom he was having an exciting affair, she a former professor of his who had encouraged him to pursue a career in microbiology, when he received a threatening text message from Lucifer himself, the message bloodcurdling but typo-ridden, and the honours graduate thought Lucifer would never have passed a single university English course if this was the best example of his writing, and as the young man thought about the older woman and how sexily she might be dressed tonight, he answered the annoying text message with GO TO HELL, spelled perfectly.

Canadian fiction writer, poet, and playwright J. J. Steinfeld lives on Prince Edward Island, where he is patiently waiting for Godot's arrival and a phone call from Kafka. While waiting, he has published fifteen books, including **Disturbing Identities** *(Stories, Ekstasis Editions),* Should the Word Hell Be Capitalized? *(Stories, Gaspereau Press),* Would You Hide Me? *(Stories, Gaspereau Press),* An Affection for Precipices *(Poetry, Serengeti Press),* **Misshapenness** *(Poetry, Ekstasis Editions),* Word Burials *(Novel and Stories, Crossing Chaos Enigmatic Ink),* A Glass Shard and Memory *(Stories, Recliner Books), and* Identity Dreams and Memory Sounds *(Poetry, Ekstasis Editions). More than three-hundred of his short stories and nearly seven-hundred poems have appeared in anthologies and periodicals internationally, and over forty of his one-act plays and a handful of full-length plays have been performed in Canada and the United States.*

The Dreamer

Denzell Cooper

Awake, I dream of darker worlds, where eldritch
Creatures wait for the living, patiently,
Aware of all who crawl the Earth above.

Asleep, I dream of waking worlds, where eldritch
Creatures shadow the living, secretly,
To steal the minds of those who find the truth.

In death, I dream of distant worlds, where eldritch
Creatures enslave the living, cruelly,
Their whips and flesh made raw until they fall,
Forgotten, chained, unloved. Asleep in death.

Denzell Cooper *lives in Cornwall, UK, where he works as a training consultant. He has written fiction, often of a dark nature, since he learnt to read, and has recently developed a love of poetry, with The Dreamer being one of his first pieces. He can be found on Twitter @DenzellCooper.*

Scorpio Gunmetal

Chris Zuver

"Help me," she whispered to the man as he slung her over his shoulder.

The man reached his arm upward toward the small crack of grey sky outside. His razor-like nails dug into the dirt above him. He pulled upward and the two of them began their ascent. As they climbed, the lightning slashed the sky open and sounds of thunder ricocheted through the pit.

He hated the weight of someone upon him, but he loved the feeling of purpose. It was such a rush, and it filled him as he dug the toes of his black suede shoes into the soil and pushed himself and the girl upward.

A pack of Beesils gathered around at the top of the lonely hill. What they were gathered around was a single grave with a freshly-dug hole. The branches of a large, graying oak tree hung perfectly still in the air. The creatures stood patiently with blind purpose in their hearts.

Beesils were two feet tall when on all fours, but seven when on their hind legs. The transformation could be made instantaneously, and they could use those two legs to run if they wanted.

The creatures didn't know where they came from. They actually only *knew* a few things and one of those was how to chase. And everyone ran once they saw their hairless bodies and horrendous faces, which always looked different every day. At this particular time, they resembled starved, thousand year-old men with black eyes and silver pupils.

The lead one nodded toward one of his lackeys and the lackey knew it was time to begin. It scooped its hand-like paw into the dirt and grabbed a large clump. It held it over the hole.

But then, everything was interrupted. With sudden immense speed, something flew out of the hole. The beast which had been digging fell backward in shock as the flash brush right past its face.

Time slowed down and the dark creatures watched helplessly. A man with a girl slung over his shoulder appeared in the branches of the tree. He wore all black, like the color of his hair. She wore a red princess dress.

He opened his mouth, but not to speak. Long ago, he had learned that speaking was overrated.

His mouth spread outward like a growing puddle. The abyss on his face grew until it was one hundred times its original size. He began to suck in air and all of the branches of the oak as well. They began to break off as he inhaled more and more of them. He simply stood there for a moment, his face an awkward and bloated shape as he began to chew.

The front Beesil was lying on its side, staring up at them. It let out a yell which sounded something like a rock being struck by the blades of a lawnmower. The girl slung over his shoulder looked on in terror.

Then, he opened his mouth again and time resumed its normal speed.

The branches launched in a scattered range, now in small chunks, set aflame. They barraged down upon the beasts, which began to dart around in a silent panic. Some of them caught fire. Their ancient flesh succumbed to the flames which spread quickly. The fallen ones flailed in mute anguish. Their eyes pried open and the entirety of the silver orbs could be seen.

The man felt the weight of the girl on his shoulder and spine.

"AIYEEE!" she screamed. Her arms tightened around him. For a brief moment, he wanted to throw her at the Beesils.

Around them, the monsters were regrouping. In the distance, he could see more of them materializing at the bottom of the hill. They simply walked into existence from out of nothingness. The ones near the bottom suddenly began bounding toward them. They gained a startling amount of ground within seconds. One leap covered half of the hill.

He had fought the Beesils a thousand times before. Each time, they took on a new face but always the same form; always the same erratic motions; always the obsession with burying their victims. He knew that they would not harm the girl, only torture her mentally. On the other hand, they would *kill* him. He leapt out of the tree and landed lightly. The, he lifted his foot and slammed it against the ground. Around them, the monsters quivered and fell onto their sides as the surface shook. The ones climbing the hill were knocked off their feet and began rolling back down.

She was the last person to have nightmares. She couldn't recall having a single one until she had heard the news from her mother two weeks ago.

"Sue, come down here. We need to talk."

She walked out of her bedroom. There was rock music ebbing through the doorway as she stepped into the hall. It only carried a few feet outward and was gone from her ears and mind before she reached the staircase. Venturing into the rest of the house was like going between dimensions. She traveled from her homely world into another that was pristine and untouched.

When she reached the living room, her mother was sitting on the couch, smoking a cigarette. She was staring into oblivion, which happened to be a few feet over the blank TV screen. As she walked in, she could see back through the kitchen to where her father stood. He was on the porch, leaning against the wall. His head was rested on his hand as he stared at the pavement. Dad never liked the smell of smoke but for some reason never asked mom to take it outside.

"Sue," went her mother.

She looked over. Mom appeared lifeless. She was still eyeing the textures in the wall.

She felt the man's feet hitting the ground as he ran. She looked up at the hairless bodies and silver eyes that were closing in around them. He turned his head back and forth and she could feel the muscles in his shoulders shifting.

It was difficult to make clear of anything. How had she gotten here? It was very unlike her to have wandered into a graveyard alone. The graveyard itself was awkwardly designed. It existed in patches. Rows of tombstones scattered the landscape around them like animal spots. She didn't remember which way she had come from.

"Where do we go now, Scorpio?" she asked the man. She trusted him. She had named him after an imaginary friend from her childhood: Scorpio Gunmetal.

"We get out of here, obviously," he replied. He was tired of answering questions like these. Saving people was merely a job now. He liked to spend his time in bitter silence, speaking only when he had to. Yet, he needed to carry on. It was too enticing not to. And besides, he was the hero, forever caught in a cycle of duty.

Things hadn't always been this way. Once, he had cared about people, but things hadn't truly been like that for time too long to fathom.

He had a unique ability. He could feel other's emotions and every impulse. He could see their fears and thoughts. Sometimes, his duty involved helping someone through a personal confrontation. This was when things would become truly invigorating. He never told them of his despondency, but he also never talked about the enjoyment either, for the fear that it would ruin the bond between them.

He had fought, befriended, and loved many times through these bonds. So was the way of his job for many years. People, victims of the Beesils or their minds own creations, would appear in his life, and stick around for a week or a month at most. He thought of himself as a "short-term hero" and it was the short-term that drove him mad, yet if the relation were to grow any longer, he figured that he would grow just as restless.

He had met the girl a week ago while she had been fleeing from a small pack of Beesils. He hadn't bothered looking at her for the most part during that week and he spoke even less. What was the point? She spent most of her time wandering through memories of her family with no threats to be seen. He hardly saw his point of guarding her most of the time. Besides, she'd be leaving him soon like the rest of them did.

While he ran down the hill, dodging ravenous monsters, he thought about these things. He thought about dropping the girl by "accident." How simple it would be.

Then, in the middle of these ponderings, a Beesil materialized some ten feet in front of him. Its face was grey and opaque like a corpse. Its jaw hung open ominously. The skin was a thousand years old the eyes spoke of certain doom and a rage it was helpless from feeding into.

The girl screamed again.

It's unnaturally large and bald body began to propel itself toward them. Its eyes grew as it came closer.

He veered around the monster and sprinted toward the bottom of the hill. Behind him, he could hear the beast turn around, ripping blades of dead grass from the ground as it did.

"Oh God! He's gaining!" she yelled.

Even if he had ever decided to throw a victim to the beasts, he thought that a part of him would never be able to let the rest do it. It was something that was too essential to him: the ability to be *something*. If he wasn't in charge of what he was doing, he would think of himself as just another drone: no different than any other *living* creature in this world. Everyone around him seemed to be single-minded all of the time. He couldn't imagine anyone other than himself and the victims having consciousness.

"Are we gonna get away?" she asked.

Are we gonna get away, he thought. *What a question.*

He thought of how audaciously the helpless clung onto his power like a mechanical bull rider grips dearly to the machine they ride. These people that needed him were completely hopeless on their own. He hated them all in that moment.

"We always do," he said quietly.

He didn't have to look at her face to know that she was silently questioning this declaration. He had saved her eight times in a row and *still* she doubted him. They were all like this and it used to not bother him.

The Beesil was gaining on him. The shadow of the creature came over them.

The girl screamed again.

He leapt up. Time slowed down. Mid-air, he turned around, gripping the girl tightly.

"Sue," spoke the Beesil in an old and deep utterance.

The sound of the creature's voice shocked him, though he didn't let it show. Rarely did the Beesils speak, and every time they did, it caught him off guard.

The creature lunged for them. Swiftly, he kicked his leg out and planted a boot in its face. It fell, landing awkwardly with feet digging into the dirt.

He turned forward again, touched back down onto the ground and continued running.

"How did you *do* that?"

"Because you're here," he said to her. She tightened her grip around him.

What he said was mostly true. He knew how to move around in his world, but a pretty trick like the one he had just managed only seemed possible while he had someone watching. It made him feel good for a moment. As time went on, though, it proved to be the only remaining thing that gave him any feeling of warmth.

Before them now, amongst the empty grey sky and grassy graves was a small red building. It resembled a caboose without wheels. The door was silver with a small handle and wide enough for two to pass through comfortably.

The girl leapt off of his back, took his hand, and ran toward it. This shift in power was typical to him. Everything was based on emotion in this world, including strength he was now pulling him. She opened the door. It was dark. There was no time to think. They passed through. The door slammed from behind.

⊰✠⊱

She looked at her mother on the couch who was keeping her eyes upon that blank void above the television. Seeing this made her feel like a car passing by on a busy street: seen but blocked out of mind.

Her mother was a skinny, dead-eyed image underneath a carefully-managed head of wavy grey hair. She held a cigarette in her mouth as she brooded.

After taking another drag, she noticed her daughter.

"Sue, sit down."

She did, feeling the foreign resistance of the love seat, which was hardly used.

"Sue. Your grandfather is dying," she said in a no bars-holed voice.

She didn't respond. She was well aware of her grandfather's lung cancer. Four times a week, for the last five months, she had paid him regular visits in the hospital. It had been one of the hardest times of her life and she had been using everything to hold herself together. It was evening now and she was exhausted, having used up all of her energy to maintain a plastic face of wellness. She now looked into the anxious eyes of her hypochondriac mother.

"I...know. I've known," she said, feeling her throat swell.

"Are you prepared for this? I mean...have you really thought about what this means?" Her voice was aggressive.

She thought about two weeks ago, when mom had gone on a rant at dinner about the dangers of headache pills and the risk of buying them after the recall. The recalls had happened after a fatal incident with a middle-aged man. The rant carried on for forty minutes. Half of the way though, dad had excused himself from the room. In the end, her mother had left, too disgusted and terrified of the world to eat. She had finished her meal in silence.

Now she didn't know what to say to her mother, except for the truth: "No. Of course I'm not."

"When was the last time we went to church, Susan?"

"I don't know."

"We'll go tomorrow. God knows you need to apologize to him."

The two of them kept walking. A small light appeared ahead, which began to grow until it was all that they could see. They shielded their eyes until they adjusted and then looked around.

They were in a church-a gothic, grandiose church. There were several people in there, all engaged in serious prayer. The clergyman stood atop the sanctuary with his hands raised to the sky and his eyes upon the floor. Behind the sanctuary, there was no wall, but an opening concealed by more intense light. It shone outwards and lit up the last rows before the church stage. Because of the people's presence, but quiet lack of attention toward the real world, an atmosphere of eerie silence was created.

The girl knew exactly what she wanted. She let go of his hand and he didn't hesitate to let her. The door behind them didn't exist anymore and Beesils weren't allowed to appear in churches or any type of spiritual place. She ran past all of the people with their heads bowed and straight into the light. The man followed in a steady walk.

The man had studied the church which she had constructed on previous visits. It was impressive. The layout was complex, reflecting her young mind. He had learned that the younger tended to overcomplicate the places that they created as a way to compensate for what they didn't know or understand.

Finally, he reached the sanctuary. The clergyman didn't move, for he was actually a statue. He turned his head forward and entered the light.

They were in a hospital ward. An old man was lying on a fold-out cot in the corner of the room. He was connected to several wires-too many for any real human. His body was frail and his skin color was fading so much that he almost looked transparent in areas. The face looked a thousand years old, all too familiar to both of them and his eyes were black with silver pupils.

He was talking, but only in whispers and only Sue was able to hear them. Nonetheless, he could feel them as they echoed through her ears:

Sue, you must come and visit me more often.

"Yes."

Maybe I'd have had a chance if you had...done that more.

"I *tried*! I tried to!" Then she was on her knees. He could feel remorse rising off of her like a rainstorm vaporizing on the surface of the sun.

The man stood there watching all of this. As he did, he felt something he hadn't in a long time: anger, genuine anger. Certainly, he had felt a lot of resentment in the past, but that had been different. As he stood there, he realized he was helpless to protect her from this type of threat: the type that claws at someone from the inside because that was exactly where it came from.

Just then, a nurse with a clipboard walked in through a door and over to the old man.

"Looks like we showed up just in time," she said.

He was tired of this. He was done with repeating the same things over and over. Also, he was tired of being charged with protecting the same people who he would often be forced to watch suffer beyond his help, and so he made a decision right there.

With one arm, he swept the girl off of the floor and ran toward the door that the nurse had left open. It had almost swung shut. He lifted his leg and extended it with swiftness, landing his ankle in the opening right before it closed. The pain was immense but he didn't have time to worry. With his free arm, he pried the door open with great effort. It seemed that the universe didn't want him to.

Behind him, he heard a growl. He glanced for a moment to see that the old man and the nurse had both transformed into Beesils and were heading straight toward them.

They bolted out of the room and into the dark. The door shut behind them.

No light appeared. There was only a sound that was familiar to the man. It sounded like a lawnmower and it was right above their heads. Then, whatever floor was beneath them fell out.

The man's heart leapt and the girl let out a scream. Then she did it again-and again-and again. It started overlapping itself as the sound repeated faster and faster. Eventually, it became one continuous sound and no longer sounded like a scream. On and on until his head began to hurt. A continuous, eternal madness seemed to be coming soon.

It stopped.

Then, he felt his legs break...followed an instant later by the rest of his body slamming into the ground.

As he lay there, he felt crushed under the force. Moments later, he could feel the bones and muscles in his legs and the rest of his body mending, but the memory of the pain stayed.

He looked over to his side, and the girl, who was lying on top of his arm, looked completely unharmed.

He decided to lie still for a moment. Any longer could be risky. The authorities of the realm already knew that he wasn't following the rules. They had left the path of the girls mind and that was forbidden. In fact, they were no longer in her mind, but they weren't in the real world, either.

She awoke, moaning lightly.

"Are you alright?" he asked.

"I'm...I'm...*fine* actually," she said, surprised. Without hesitation, she pushed herself back up.

For the man, it took a moment longer to get to his feet. He felt frustration and a little bit of shock. He had never been off of the path before.

He looked around. There was nothing but blackness and the girl. He could see his body and hers, as if they were receiving perfect lighting, but everything else was a backdrop of nothing.

The girl was looking at him, confused as usual.

"What now?" she asked.

"You follow me."

And so she did. For ten minutes, she followed him through the abyss. He honestly had no idea where he was going. He was   certain that he was being toyed with. Somebody had to be watching to have healed his legs and keep the girl from harm. It was only a matter of time until...

Then, and not unlike when they had entered the church, a small light appeared ahead in the distance. It was not pure light this time, but some type of object. He broke into a run, unconcerned with whether or not the girl was keeping up.

He kept running until he was within a few feet of the object the stopped. He stared in thought for a moment. It was a couch-a canapé to be precise. Its light-green leather contrasted awkwardly against the black world around it. He heard the girl walk up from behind and stop next to him.

"What is this?" she asked.

Without looking at her, he shook his head

Another light slowly appeared beyond the canapé. What started as a speck slowly grew until it took the form of a person. The light faded and in its place stood a tall, thin man. He wore a dark blue suit and his head was shaved, although grey stubble was visible. He stood rigidly facing them with a smirk.

"Good evening, Scorpio. Good evening, Susan. Please sit down."

They did.

His eyes were upon the girl. "I'm sorry that there have been some minor issues. Scorpio and I must take care of something quickly. You will be taken care of very soon."

Scorpio suddenly felt the compulsion to blink. He did and then he saw that the girl was gone.

"Scorpio. Scorpio *Gunmetal*...now that's an interesting name she gave you. What seems to be the problem?" His tone sounded genuinely curious, something he hadn't expected.

The apparition cracked his knuckles and folded his arms. He began to feel uncomfortable. He wanted to tell the tall man what he came for and he needed to know what his reply would be. It was as simple as that. No need for pleasantries.

"I already know what you want," spoke the tall man. "Decades ago, you came to me and asked for unlimited life. This is what you get. Don't you remember?"

He thought about it. He twisted his mind back and forth trying to recall anything, but could think of no memories that the man described.

"No," he said, suddenly feeling upset. "Why *would* I? If there was ever anything before constantly having to lose friendships and loves then those losses have made it impossible to remember."

"A bit dramatic, don't you think? You need to appreciate the opportunity you have. Think of all of those great people that have been strewn along your path. Most people go their entire lives without having even one *true* love and they *may* have a decent friendship or two. This is the beauty of what I have given you."

"What are you talking about?"

"If most people only have a couple friends in their lives and I've let you have ten *thousand*, then you're well on your way to living *eternally*."

He thought about this for a moment. The tall man was tapping his fingers on the sleeves of his shirt. His eyes were calm, but losing patience.

It's just the opposite," he said. "Living is constantly working at something. I've done nothing but lose since I've come here."

The tall man looked at him and shook his head. "If you don't like my lesson, then I can't help you anymore."

"What are you going to do then?"

"I'm going to send you on one more job. Kill the girl and you'll go free."

He widened his eyes. "You can't be serious."

"Quite. I'll put you near her so it will be easy."

"I won't."

"If you want to be free, then you will."

He blinked, and the man that the girl called Scorpio was gone.

Chris Zuver *was born and raised around St. Charles County. In-between sleeping and sleeping, he plays in his band and gets on everyone's nerves (not necessarily because of his band). He hopes to one day be successful in art, regardless of what type it is.*

JEALOUS STONE

Florence Grey

I envy them,
their eternal slumber and long stilled silence —

Unlike my own loud, chaotic existence, I ache
to lay my weary head upon their graves,
to let my fingers trace over weathered stone,
worn down not by worry but by time —

to absorb their peaceful silence and earthly constitution,
to scream until my lungs resonate the grassy, hallowed ground
for which my jealousy now lays cold.

Florence Grey *has been writing poetry for nearly twenty years. She loves the swing and big band era and prefers writing her poetry with pen and paper to that of a computer.*

www.ingramcontent.com/pod-product-compliance
Lightning Source LLC
Chambersburg PA
CBHW071216130626
46555CB00004B/1729